To my sisters, Madeleine and Lucille,
in remembrance of our unique bicycle
—P. D.

For you, little baby, who appeared in
my tummy during the creation
of this book
—Orbie

MARGARET K. McELDERRY BOOKS
An imprint of Simon & Schuster Children's Publishing Division
1230 Avenue of the Americas, New York, New York 10020
Text copyright © 2014 by Pierrette Dubé
Illustrations copyright © 2014 by Orbie
English language translation copyright © 2018 by Simon & Schuster, Inc.
Originally published in Canada in 2014 by *Les Éditions Les 400 coups* as *La petite truie, le vélo et la lune*
All rights reserved, including the right of reproduction in whole or in part in any form.
MARGARET K. McELDERRY BOOKS is a trademark of Simon & Schuster, Inc.
For information about special discounts for bulk purchases, please contact Simon & Schuster Special Sales at 1-866-506-1949
or business@simonandschuster.com.
The Simon & Schuster Speakers Bureau can bring authors to your live event. For more information or to book an event,
contact the Simon & Schuster Speakers Bureau at 1-866-248-3049 or visit our website at www.simonspeakers.com.
Book design by Sonia Chaghatzbanian and Irene Metaxatos
The text for this book was set in Calisto MT and Chalkduster.
Manufactured in China
0718 SCP
First Edition
2 4 6 8 10 9 7 5 3 1
Library of Congress Cataloging-in-Publication Data
Names: Dubé, Pierrette, 1952– author. | Orbie 1984– illustrator.
Title: The little pig, the bicycle, and the moon / Pierrette Dubé; illustrated by: Orbie.
Other titles: Petite truie, le vélo et la lune. English
Description: First edition. | New York : Margaret K. McElderry Books, [2018] | Summary: "Rosie is a little pig determined to
learn how to ride a bike and see the world, no matter how many mishaps it takes for her to get there!"—Provided by publisher.
Identifiers: LCCN 2018000238 (print) | LCCN 2017054182 (eBook)
ISBN 9781534414723 (hardcover) | ISBN 9781534414730 (eBook)
Subjects: | CYAC: Pigs—Fiction. | Bicycles and bicycling—Fiction. | Determination (Personality trait)—Fiction. | Domestic
animals—Fiction.
Classification: LCC PZ7.D84923 (print) | LCC PZ7.D84923 Lit 2018 (eBook) | DDC [E]—dc23
LC record available at https://lccn.loc.gov/2018000238

THE LITTLE PIG, THE BICYCLE, AND THE MOON

BY Pierrette Dubé

ART BY Orbie

MARGARET K. McELDERRY BOOKS

New York London Toronto Sydney New Delhi

ROSIE, the little pig, had everything she needed to be happy: a large mud bath to play in, enough food to eat whenever she wanted, and a deliciously smelly pigpen.

Play, eat, sleep . . . The little pig wanted nothing more.

Until the day a red bicycle appeared in the
yard. To her it was a pure wonder.

It was ridden by a small, very ugly animal
that had no snout or curly tail.

Rosie spent hours watching
the small animal on the bicycle.

One night, the little pig quietly snuck out of the pigpen.

The yard was empty. Everyone was asleep except Rosie and the moon.

You can watch if you want to, Moon.

The bicycle, leaning against a wall, seemed to be waiting
for Rosie. The little pig got onto the bike, started to pedal . . .

but **BONK!** The bicycle fell on its side.

She tried several times, but the same thing happened.

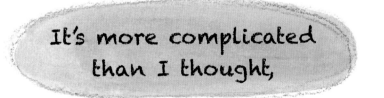

It's more complicated
than I thought,

said Rosie.

There is probably something I'm
doing wrong, but what?

The next day, she again watched the small animal on the bicycle.
To start, he gave a good push with his foot.

So that's the trick.

I'll get it. And when I know how to pedal, I'll go to the other side of the world, and maybe even farther. . . .

The next night, Rosie dragged the bicycle up a hill, thinking that would make it easier to gain speed. She was right. The bicycle took off, rolled a few yards, then began to zigzag . . .

and **BOOM!** It crashed into the side of the henhouse.

The hens, awakened by the noise, were dying of laughter. How humiliating!

A little shaken, Rosie decided
it would be safer to wear a helmet.

When she arrived the next night, the entire
barnyard was already there, waiting for the show.
The moon was there too, and Rosie felt as if it
were watching over her, like a friend.

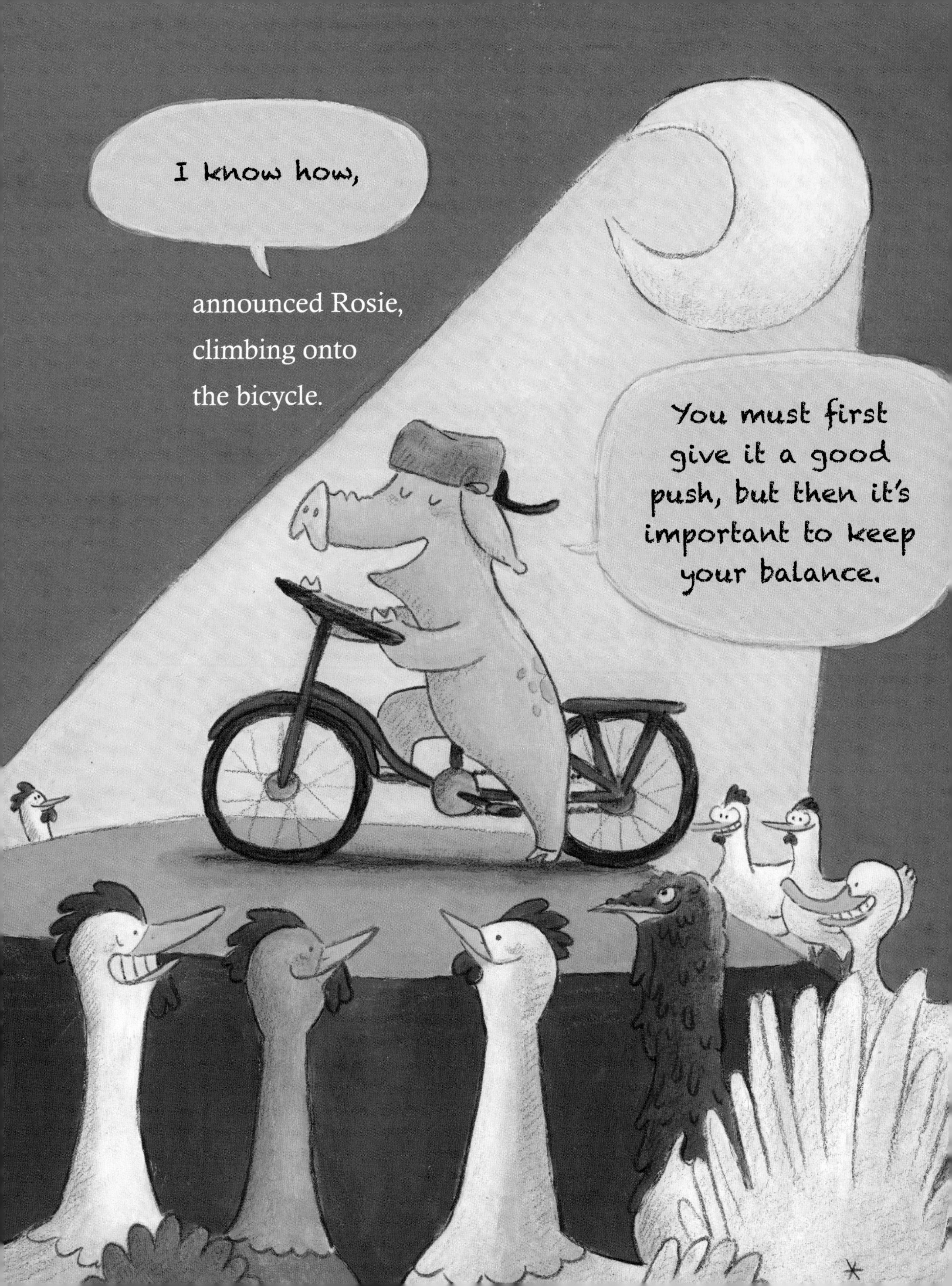

announced Rosie, climbing onto the bicycle.

Rosie started down the sloped path
that led to the pond, while the chickens
followed her, cackling.

She made it down the hill without losing
her balance, but she couldn't make the turn
just before the pond, and . . .

SPLASH!

Rosie was in the water
with the bicycle.

What's that? Man overboard?

shouted the dog.

She wants to ride a bike,

answered the chattiest hen.

It will never happen,

gobbled the turkey.

The dog looked at Rosie with sympathy.

Cycling is certainly an action-packed sport,

thought Rosie,

but it's so much fun!

The next night, she put on her protective equipment, adding to it, for extra safety, a rubber tire and a snorkel.

The dog was waiting for her, as promised.

I will pull you.

He harnessed himself to the bicycle and pulled. The bicycle quickly gained speed.

But suddenly a rabbit crossed the yard,
running toward the vegetable garden.
The dog could not resist the temptation
to chase it.

And Rosie landed on her back,
between the tomato plants and
the leeks.

Rosie now added a new piece of equipment:
a cushion, in case of falls into the garden. With
her new outfit, she felt invincible.

This time,
I'm completely
ready.

It's not enough to
give yourself a good
push and then keep
your balance.

You also have
to know how to
turn and put on
the brakes.

That night,
the goat was called
in to help.

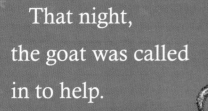

She planted her horns and rushed
straight ahead while Rosie pedaled
furiously.

After a few minutes, the little pig
turned around and was astonished to
see that the goat was gone.

The moon had never been
as bright as it was that night. . . .

You see, Moon.
I did it!

Thrilled, the little pig pedaled with
all her might.

She braked in front of the gate,
opened it, turned right, rode up the hill,

CREAK

and disappeared into the moonlight. . . .

What became of her? No one knows. Some say she pedaled and pedaled without stopping until she reached the other side of the world.

They say she now works in the circus, where her performance is very famous.

Others say that the other side of the world wasn't far enough for Rosie, and if you look up high when the sky is clear, you can sometimes see a little pig on a red bicycle, pedaling on the moon.

Cluck!

Cluck?